Savannah's Bandanas

by Jeryl Christmas

This Book Belongs To

_____

This book is dedicated to all of the educators and students facing the challenges of the 2020-21 school year.

Savannah's bandanas are all laid out.

She has a school collection.

Each one serves the purpose

of providing her protection.

She really doesn't mind them,

but they seem a little bleak

since they cover up her smile

and the dimple on her cheek!

"Your smile is **very** special,"

her gram would always say.

"Sometimes just a simple smile

can make a person's day."

But Savannah's smile is hidden,

so how can she display

grins for her friends

in a **different** sort of way?

She'll need to be creative

when going back to school

in how to safely follow

this necessary rule.

She'll pick the perfect fabrics

with prints that make her smile

and cut out **new** bandanas

to brighten up her style.

She'll look for cheerful things

like a kitty cat or pup—

something to spread joy

since her smile is covered up.

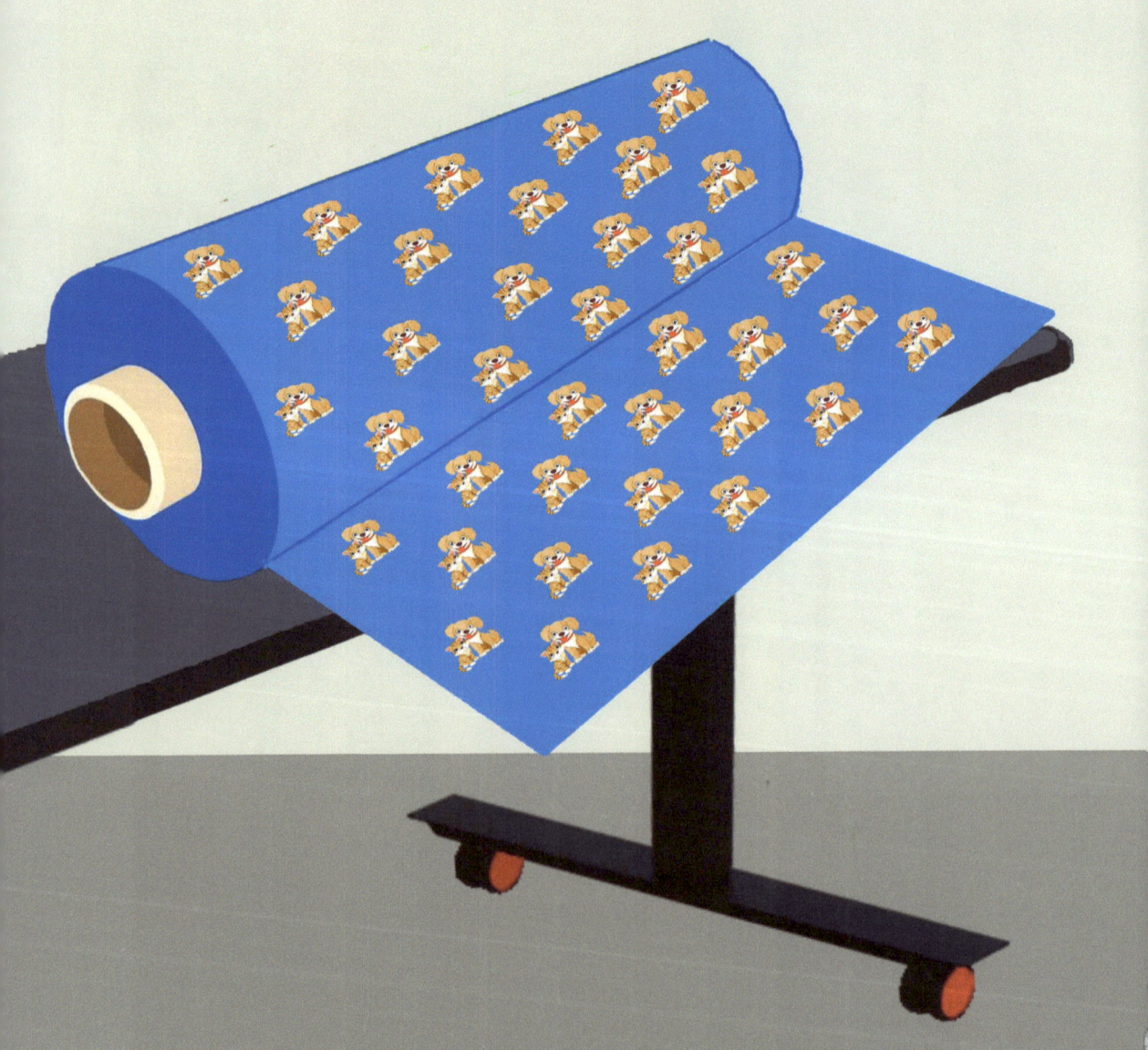

Bandanas showing butterflies

flying in the air

will comfort and console

like a favorite teddy bear.

The last year ended suddenly

when schools came to a halt.

Teachers couldn't say good-bye,

but it was no one's fault.

Savannah gave her teacher

bright balloons to bring her cheer.

Her thank you smile could not be seen,

but she could see the tear.

This new year **will** bring changes.

Each child will have more space,

but every teacher's going to miss

that first day's warm embrace.

Bumping elbows will be done

with hugging in the air.

This will be the **new** way

for folks to show they care.

P.E. may be at recess—

other specials in the room,

but these students will adjust.

They're the ones who learned to ...

ZOOM!

No other class has ever

been as challenged as this group.

Technology and teachers

kept their students in the loop.

Devices were delivered.

Their buses brought them lunch!

People worked **together**

like they do when in a crunch.

Regardless of the class,

no matter what the grade,

Savannah says **no** student

should ever be afraid.

The teachers will assure them

as they start a brand new year ...

Learning will resume again

without a need to fear.

So when your smile is covered,

try to grin **another** way

by spreading joy and kindness

like Savannah did each day.

This class will be remembered

for many years to come.

The class of '21

will **NEVER** be outdone!

THE END

www.ingramcontent.com/pod-product-compliance
Lightning Source LLC
Chambersburg PA
CBHW041009170626
46815CB00002B/223